Note to parents, carers and teachers

Read it yourself is a series of modern stories, favourite characters and traditional tales written in a simple way for children who are learning to read. The books can be read independently or as part of a guided reading session.

Each book is carefully structured to include many high-frequency words vital for first reading. The sentences on each page are supported closely by pictures to help with understanding, and to offer lively details to talk about.

The books are graded into four levels that progressively introduce wider vocabulary and longer stories as a reader's ability and confidence grows.

Ideas for use

- Begin by looking through the book and talking about the pictures. Has your child heard this story before?

- Help your child with any words he does not know, either by helping him to sound them out or supplying them yourself.

- Developing readers can be concentrating so hard on the words that they sometimes don't fully grasp the meaning of what they're reading. Answering the puzzle questions on pages 30 and 31 will help with understanding.

For more information and advice on Read it yourself and book banding, visit www.ladybird.com/readityourself

Book
Band
5

Level 1 is ideal for children who have received some initial reading instruction. Each story is told very simply, using a small number of frequently repeated words.

Special features:

Opening pages introduce key story words

Careful match between story and pictures

Large, clear type

parrot

Dad Mummy

giraffe

lion

polar bear

Tim

Topsy

zebra

7

seal

monkey

penguin

6

Topsy and Tim liked to go to the zoo with Mummy and Dad.

They liked to see all the animals.

8

9

Educational Consultant: Geraldine Taylor
Book Banding Consultant: Kate Ruttle

Written by Lorraine Horsley
Illustrated by Belinda Worsley

A catalogue record for this book is available from the British Library

Published by Ladybird Books Ltd
80 Strand, London, WC2R 0RL
A Penguin Company

002

ISBN: 978-0-72327-372-1

Printed in China

Topsy and Tim
Go to the Zoo

By Jean and Gareth Adamson

parrot

Dad

Mummy

Tim

Topsy

seal

monkey

6

giraffe

lion

polar bear

zebra

penguin

Topsy and Tim liked to go to the zoo with Mummy and Dad.

They liked to see all the animals.

First, they went to see
the penguins.

"Can we have a penguin for
a pet?" asked Topsy and Tim.

"No!" said Mummy.

Next, they went to see
the parrots.

"Can we have a parrot for
a pet?" asked Topsy and Tim.

"No!" said Dad.

Next, they went to see the giraffes.

"Can we have a giraffe for a pet?" asked Topsy and Tim.

"No!" said Mummy.

Next, they went to see
the zebras.

"Can we have a zebra
for a pet?" asked Topsy
and Tim.

"No!" said Dad.

Next, they went to see the polar bears.

"Can we have a polar bear for a pet?" asked Topsy and Tim.

"No!" said Mummy.

Next, they went to see
the lions.

"Can we have a lion for
a pet?" asked Topsy and Tim.

"No!" said Dad.

Next, they went to see
the seals.

"Can we have a seal for
a pet?" asked Topsy and Tim.

"No!" said Mummy.

Next, they went to
see the monkeys.

"Can we have a monkey for
a pet?" asked Topsy and Tim.

"No!" said Dad.

Topsy and Tim went home.

"I liked all the animals at the zoo," said Topsy.

"With all these pets, we have a zoo at home!" said Dad.

How much do you remember about the story of Topsy and Tim: Go to the Zoo? Answer these questions and find out!

- Which animals do Topsy and Tim see first?

- What are the lions eating?

- How many pets do Topsy and Tim have?

Look at the pictures from the story and say the order they should go in.

A

B

C

D

Answer: C, D, A, B.

Read it yourself with Ladybird

Second

Tick the books you've read!

For children who are ready to take their first steps in reading

Level 1

 The Enormous Turnip ☐

 Fairy Friends ☐

 Goldilocks and the Three Bears ☐

 Little Red Hen ☑

 The Magic Porridge Pot ☑

 Little Creatures ☐

 Recycling Fun! ☐

 The Princess and the Pea ☐

 Cinderella ☐

 Rex the Big Dinosaur ☐

 The Tale of Peter Rabbit ☐

 The Three Billy Goats Gruff ☐

 Why Giraffe has a Long Neck ☐

 Topsy and Tim Go to the Zoo ☑

 The Ugly Duckling ☐

 The Emperor's New Clothes ☐

For beginner readers who can read short, simple sentences with help.

Level 2

 Beauty and the Beast ☐

 Chicken Licken ☐

 Little Red Riding Hood ☐

 Nature Trail ☐

 Sports Day ☐

 Pirate School ☐

 Rumpelstiltskin ☐

 Sleeping Beauty ☐

 The Gingerbread Man ☐

 Sly Fox and Red Hen ☐

 The Tale of Jemima Puddle-Duck ☐

 The Three Little Pigs ☐

 Why Lion Roarrrs! ☐

 Topsy and Tim The Big Race ☐

 Town Mouse and Country Mouse ☐

 Dom's Dragon ☐

 Available on the App Store

The Read it yourself with Ladybird app is now available for iPad, iPhone and iPod touch

App also available on Android devices